For Thomas and Charlie

The fireworks had fizzled, the bonfires, just embers,
The snow on the ground, it was nearly December.

With twinkling lights and jingling bells in the air,
The excitement was rising, he soon would be there.

But one little girl couldn't muster much cheer,
Not when she knew he wouldn't come here.
Not to the new house, she knew this was true,
It just seemed impossible, there was nothing to do.

She had searched her new home, every nook, every cranny
She had looked in the cupboards, she'd even asked Granny.

But to her dismay, the fact remained clear,
Without a big fireplace, he couldn't come near.

She'd listened to stories at home and at school,
Each one of the tales followed one simple rule...

On Christmas Eve night, before closing your eyes,
To the fireplace you go, to leave your mince pies.

And as you are sleeping on that cold winter's night,
Down the chimney comes Santa, his eyes gleaming bright.

And ever so quietly, whilst the house was all still,
He'd eat the mince pie and the stockings he'd fill.

Oh, how magical, the tales made it seem,
But without a big chimney it was all just a dream.

"Write your letter" said Dad "or your chance will be missed,
Father Christmas needs time to work on your list."

With tears in her eyes, her voice timid and small,
She explained, with no chimney, there was no point at all.
Dad looked very thoughtful, he shared her dismay.
"You write your letter and I'll find a way".

As Christmas approached, the days would not slow,
The nativity at school and the pantomime show.
Decorating the tree and skating on ice,
The Christmassy smells of apple and spice.

Gingerbread houses and striped candy canes,
Holly on wreaths and cold snowy lanes.
Carols and parties, all in good cheer,
The feeling that's saved for this time of year.

Christmas Eve had arrived, every child was excited,
It had finally come, they all were delighted.

All except one, her worry was mounting,
To help make her smile, Dad planned an outing.

With no idea where she was, she looked all around,
Decorations, bright lights and snow on the ground.
Reindeer stood patiently, in front of the sleigh,
Elves with big smiles, loading presents away.

A sign on the lane said follow the light,
She clutched her Dad's hand in excitement and fright.
A log cabin was nestled amid Christmas Tree lighting,
A glow from the window, warm and inviting.

Out stepped a figure, his face lit with cheer,
He beckoned them in, there was nothing to fear

The North Pole

As they stepped through the door to Santa's small lair,
He sat himself down and offered a chair.

"Now, I have your letter, I've read it twice through,
I see you've been worried, this simply won't do."

"I want to assure you, when chimneys aren't there
I have other ways, my secret I'll share."

"All that you need, for a visit from me,
Is kindness and magic... and this special key."

From his pocket he took a box wrapped with a bow,
He offered it to her, her cheeks were aglow.

"Just tie the red ribbon to your door - make it tight,
I'll see it's strong glow in the cold winter light."

She looked at her Dad, a smile on her face,
"Come Dad, be quick, we've no time to waste!"

A blanket of snow, lit by the moon,
Bedtime was calling, the visit was soon.
The mince pies took their place, at the foot of the tree,
The key fixed in place, as tight as can be.

With one last look out the window, full of wonder and joy,
She shared the excitement of each girl and boy.
As she closed her eyes tight, dreams filling her mind,
The sleigh flew through the sky, not one child left behind.

The icy blue light of a cold Christmas dawn,
crept through the room as she awoke with a yawn.

As she flew down the stairs, feet barely touching the floor,
She burst into the room then stopped, full of awe.

Her stocking was bursting, gifts under the tree,
And sitting so proudly, her gold magic key.

Next to the key, his writing so clear,
"Merry Christmas" it said "See you next year".

Made in United States
North Haven, CT
13 December 2021

12674350R00020